D0500960

Benjamin Bigfoot

by Mary Serfozo
illustrated by Jos. A. Smith

MARGARET K. McELDERRY BOOKS • New York

Maxwell Macmillan Canada • Toronto

Maxwell Macmillan International • New York • Oxford • Singapore • Sydney

Margaret K. McElderry Books
Macmillan Publishing Company, 866 Third Avenue, New York, NY 10022
Maxwell Macmillan Canada, Inc., 1200 Eglinton Avenue East, Suite 200, Don Mills, Ontario M3C 3N1
Macmillan Publishing Company is part of the Maxwell Communication Group of Companies.

First edition. Printed in Hong Kong by South China Printing Company (1988) Ltd.
The text of this book is set in Galliard. The illustrations are rendered in watercolor, pen and pencil.
10 9 8 7 6 5 4 3 2 1

Library of Congress Cataloging-in-Publication Data
Serfozo, Mary.
Benjamin Bigfoot / by Mary Serfozo ; illustrated by Jos. A. Smith.
—1st ed.   p.   cm.
Summary: Because he feels big when he wears his father's shoes, a little boy wants to wear them
when he begins kindergarten.
ISBN 0-689-50570-1
[1. Kindergarten—Fiction. 2. Schools—Fiction. 3. Shoes—Fiction.]   I. Smith, Joseph A.
(Joseph Anthony), date, ill. II. Title.   PZ7.S482Be 1993   [E]—dc20   92-321

For Steve and Dave, Deb I and Deb II
                                        —M.S.

For my friends, Andrea L., who learns
things faster than I ever could, and
Charissa, for going back to school.
                                        —J.A.S.

These are Benjamin's feet.

And these are Benjamin's shoes. (They used to belong to his dad.)

Benjamin calls them his "big shoes," and
when he tugs them on over his sneakers,
then he feels big, too.

He splash, splash, splashes through puddles

And crunch, crunch, crunches through snow.

He oozes through mud

And scuffles through dust

And ruffles through piles of dried leaves.

He can make great, big footprints, or
slide along with no footprints at all.

And it's almost as much fun as having someone to play with.

But not quite.

So Benjamin was getting more and more excited as it got closer to the day when he'd start kindergarten.

"I'll have to have a lunch box," he said.

"And new pants and shirts too," agreed his mother.

"But I already have my big shoes," said
Benjamin.

"Oh," said his mother. "I don't think you
want to wear your *big* shoes to school."

"Yes, I do," replied Benjamin. "Of course
I do." (School was one place where he
knew he would want to feel big.)

"No one else will be wearing big shoes, probably," said his mother.

"I won't care," said Benjamin.

"Schools have rules, you know," said his mother. "They may have one about shoes."

Benjamin didn't know what to say. It was such a big school and he wouldn't know anyone there at all.

"If I can't wear my big shoes," he said at last, "I guess maybe I won't go to school after all."

His mother looked surprised. "Oh, that would be too bad," she said, "after you've waited all this time. Well, we'll just have to see."

The next day when Benjamin was outside
playing his mother called, "Come on, let's
go for a ride. Leave your big shoes on, if
you want to."

They drove down out of the woods where Benjamin lived, and his mother stopped the car in front of the school.

"It's all right if we just go in and look around," she said. "I talked with the kindergarten teacher this morning and she said she'd be here getting things ready."

Miss Castle was in the classroom hanging up pictures, and she smiled at Benjamin when he came in. "You're just the man I need," she said, handing him the end of a paper chain. "Would you climb up the little ladder and hold this for me?"

Benjamin tried, but his big shoes wouldn't
fit and the ladder went over with a crash.

"Never mind," said Miss Castle. "Come
on out and see the playground."

Benjamin looked at the climbing dome,
then he looked at his big shoes.

"I'm a good climber," he said.

"I'm sure you are," Miss Castle answered.

Benjamin tried one of the bikes

and the slide

and the balance bar, but his shoes kept
getting in the way.

Miss Castle didn't seem to notice.

She showed him where the class jumped
rope and ran races and played tag.

"I can run fast, too," Benjamin said,
"when I'm not wearing my big shoes."

"I'd like to see you run," said Miss Castle,
"when you're not wearing your big shoes."

Then it was time to go, and Miss Castle smiled at Benjamin again and said she hoped he'd be coming back when school started. And by then he knew he wanted to come back more than he'd ever wanted anything before.

On the way home he said to his mother, "You know, I've been thinking. Maybe I *could* go to school without my big shoes."

"Do you really think so?" asked his mother.

"Well, it's only for a couple of hours every day. And I could still wear them at home whenever I wanted."

"That's true," agreed his mother.

"And they don't have any good puddles or leaves or mud on the school grounds, anyway."

"Also true," said his mother.

"Besides, there are probably some things I could learn in school," Benjamin said. "And I'd have lots of new friends to play with."

"Yes, you would," said his mother.

"And Miss Castle must be the nicest
teacher in the whole school."

"I wouldn't be surprised," said his mother.

Then Benjamin began to smile.

His mother began to smile, too.

And they just went right on smiling
all the way home.